TABLE OF CONTENTS

IMAGES
The Earth

Concept:
Émilie Beaumont

Text:
Agnès Vandewiele

Illustrations:
S. Alloy, C. David, F. Guiraud,
P. Bon, F. Ruyer

Translation:
Lara M. Andahazy

FLEURUS

OUR PLACE
IN THE UNIVERSE

THE BIG BANG

The universe that we live in was created by a huge explosion that scientists call the "Big Bang."

The Big Bang sent a very large amount of very hot matter out into space.

Scientists think that this happened around 15 billion years ago.

The bits of matter spat out in the explosion formed a cloud of dust that began to rotate.

THE GALAXIES

The bits of matter in the cloud grouped together while it was turning and formed stars.

These stars formed huge plate-like groups called galaxies. Galaxies come in different shapes.

Earth is in a galaxy called the Milky Way. It looks like a plate from the side. The sun and Earth are near the edge.

HOW THE EARTH WAS FORMED

The earth was formed four and a half to five billion years ago out of the cloud of gases and dust from the Big Bang.

The dust clumped together as it whirled about and formed Earth and the other planets.

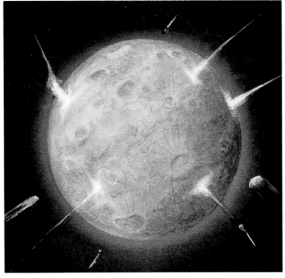

The earth was then bombarded by a storm of meteorites that dug huge craters.

3.9 billion years ago the earth was flooded by a huge storm. Water filled the craters which became lakes and oceans.

THE SOLAR SYSTEM

The solar system is made up of our sun and the nine planets that move around it. The sun is a bright star in the center.

The nine planets are: Mercury (1), Venus (2), Earth (3), Mars (4), Jupiter (5), Saturn (6), Uranus (7), Neptune (8) and Pluto (9). The planets closest to the sun turn the fastest; the furthest planets move more slowly.

WHAT SHAPE IS THE EARTH?

In ancient times, we thought that the earth was flat and round, like a plate, and floated on the oceans around it.

The first navigators thought the edges of the seas fell off into nothingness.

Ferdinand Magellan was the first to sail all the way around the world.

Earth is shaped like a ball that is slightly flattened at the top and bottom.

Earth spins like a top. The big circle around its middle is the equator.

HOW BIG IS THE EARTH?

You would have to travel 24,900 miles to go all the way around the earth. That is almost ten times the distance from San Francisco to New York!

If you walked for ten hours a day, it would take you 2 years to go around the world.

If you drove a car 10 hours a day at 60 miles per hour, it would take you 40 days.

It would take an airplane almost two days to fly around the world.

The space shuttle can fly around the world in one and a half hours.

THE BLUE PLANET

Earth is called the blue planet because most of the surface of the planet is covered with water. Earth is all blue when seen from space!

There are five oceans and hundreds of seas on Earth. The biggest and deepest is the Pacific Ocean.

Here is a picture of Earth as seen from space. The crew on the space shuttle has a great view of our planet during its missions!

THE AIR AROUND US

A 500-mile-thick layer of air called the atmosphere surrounds our planet. The atmosphere makes life on Earth possible.

Plants need air and water in order to grow.

When it is cold out, you can see the air that comes out of your mouth.

The air is thinner on high mountain tops; it can be hard to breathe up high.

The layer of air around Earth protects us from the sun's rays.

THE EARTH MOVES AROUND THE SUN

Like the other planets, Earth moves in a big circle around the sun.
It goes around the sun once every year (365 days).

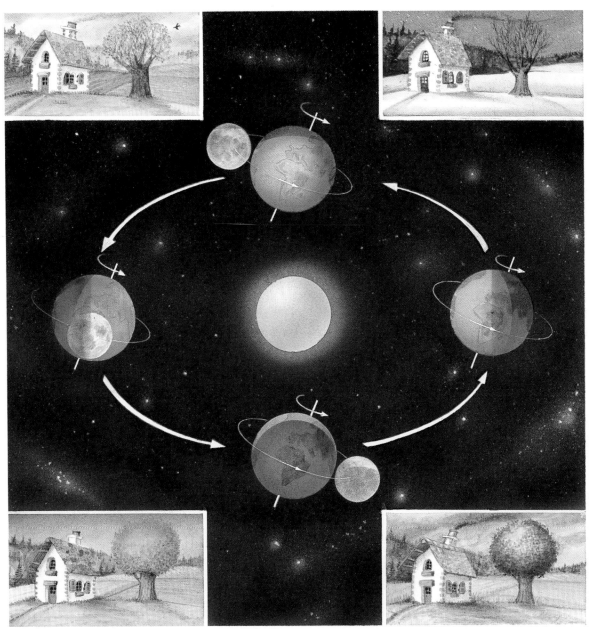

When the sun's rays shine straight at us it is summer and the weather is warm. When they shine at an angle it is winter and the weather is cold.

ONE DAY

The earth spins like a top. It takes Earth 24 hours (one day) to spin all the way around once.

Find the red dot—it's in Europe. It has just left the shady area. It is morning there.

The sun is right in front of Europe so it is noon there.

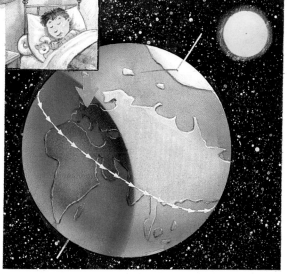

As Earth turns, Europe will move into the shady area where the sun's rays can't reach it.

Now Europe is in the shade and Earth hides the sun's rays. It is nighttime.

THE FOUR CORNERS OF THE WORLD

At the same moment, in the four corners of the world, these children are doing different things because it is not the same time of day for them.

Ben is getting up. It is 8 AM in New York.

Elodie is eating lunch. It is 1 PM in Paris.

In China, Han is getting ready for bed. It is evening.

Joanna is sleeping. It is the middle of the night in Australia.

THE TWELVE MONTHS OF THE YEAR

One month (28 to 31 days) is about the time it takes the moon to go around the earth one time (29 1/2 days).

Every year the moon goes around the earth 12 times. That's why the year is divided into 12 months. There are 4 seasons that last 3 months each. Can you point to the beginning and end of each season on the picture above?

HOW WAS YOUR DAY?

The sun's position in the sky changes during the day. Where is the sun while we do each of these things?

When we wake up.

When we eat lunch.

When we eat dinner.

When we are sleeping.

The sun is high in the sky.

The sun is setting.

Night.

The sun is rising.

HAPPY BIRTHDAY!

Benjamin is 5 years old today. That means that the earth has gone around the sun five times since he was born. His birthday cake has a candle for each year on it. How many times has the earth gone around the sun since you were born? What month is your birthday?

SEASONS

Seasons are times of the year when the weather is pretty much the same and the temperature does not change much. But, not every country has the same number of seasons.

There are two seasons—winter and summer—at the poles. Each for 6 months.

There are two seasons in the savannah, too: a dry season and a rainy season.

There are no seasons at the equator. It is hot and rains every day.

There are four seasons in areas where it is not too hot or too cold.

THE FOUR SEASONS

We live in a temperate climate. It is not too hot or too cold.
Four seasons follow each other every year.

Spring: the days get longer and the sun shines more and more. Trees start to bloom.

Summer: the days are long, the sun shines and it is hot. Fruit ripens on the trees.

Autumn: the days get shorter, the sky is gray and it is rainy and windy a lot. The leaves fall.

Winter: the days are short, it is cold and it snows. The trees have lost all their leaves.

23

CHRISTMAS IN SUMMER?!

Many children celebrate Christmas in the summer! In Brazil, south of the equator, December 25 is in summer. But in the United States it is winter.

Jane has decorated her Christmas tree and hung up her stocking. It is Christmas morning and it is snowing outside. She and her little brother are opening the presents that Santa Claus left under their tree.

At the same time, in Brazil, Claudio and his little sister are opening their presents. Santa Claus brought them last night. It is very hot and sunny out. They might go on a picnic in the park with their parents later.

HOT AND COLD, HOT AND COLD

The climate on Earth is always changing. 16,000 years ago northern Europe was covered in ice. Then, it got warmer. What might happen in the future?

The climate is getting hotter and desert winds might cover cities in Africa with sand in about 50 years.

But, in a few centuries it might get cold again and ice could cover North America. New York could be buried in ice.

CLIMATES

The temperature in different areas of the world is called the climate.
There are many different climates.

In temperate climates the weather is mild. It is not too hot or too cold.

Inland, far from the coast, winters are colder and summers are hotter.

In the desert, days are very hot and nights are cool. It hardly ever rains.

It is never very cold in this tropical forest. Dry periods follow heavy rains.

An area's climate depends on its position in relation to the poles (where it is coldest) and the equator (where it is hottest). The altitude and the distance from an ocean also affect the climate.

In India, torrential rains flood the streets. It's the monsoon season.

This village is just south of the equator. It is hot all year but it rains every day.

Winters are cold and snowy in the mountains. Summers are hot and stormy.

Winters are long and freezing near the poles. Summers are cold and short.

QUESTION EARTH
Try to answer these questions on your own.

The Big Bang was:
– an explosion
– a huge star
– a galaxy

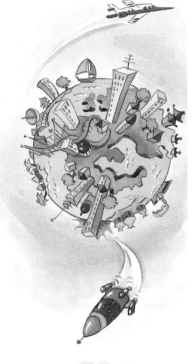

What shape is Earth?
– round like a ball
– flat like a plate

The earth rotates once in:
– a year
– a day

One year is:
– the time it takes the earth
to go around the sun
– the time it takes the moon
to go around the earth

LANDFORMS
AND ROCKS

WHAT IS INSIDE THE EARTH?

Earth is like a big piece of fruit. It has a skin, the crust, a fleshy part, the mantle, and a pit, the core, in the center.

It is 3,963 miles from the surface of the earth to the center.

The crust is very thin, about 6 miles deep in most places. It is a layer of rock that floats on the mantle.

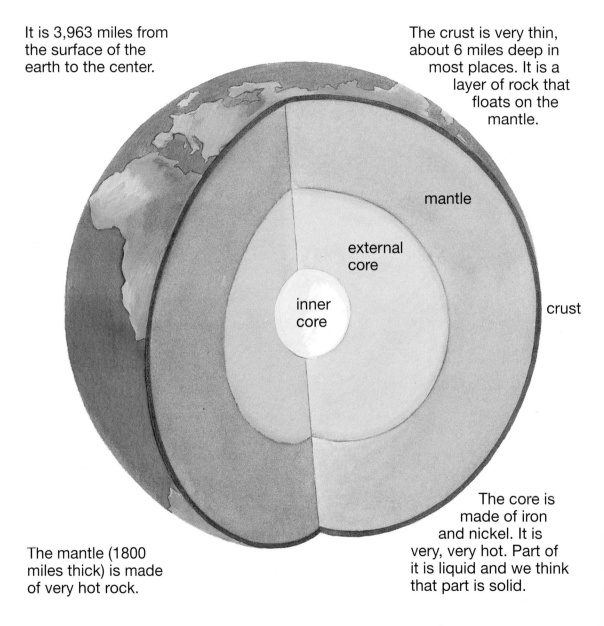

mantle

external core

inner core

crust

The mantle (1800 miles thick) is made of very hot rock.

The core is made of iron and nickel. It is very, very hot. Part of it is liquid and we think that part is solid.

A very long time ago, Earth was a ball of fire. The surface cooled down but the center is still burning hot.

FLOATING CONTINENTS

The continents sit on huge plates of the earth's crust. These plates move slowly (about 1 inch per year) and move the continents.

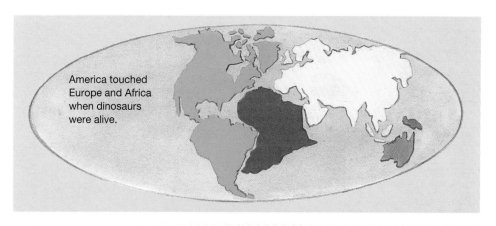

America touched Europe and Africa when dinosaurs were alive.

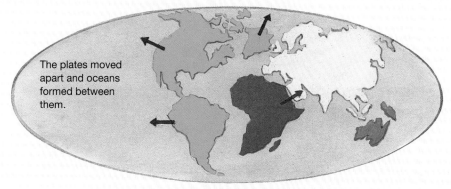

The plates moved apart and oceans formed between them.

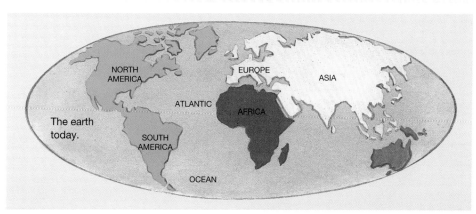

The earth today.

NORTH AMERICA · EUROPE · ASIA · ATLANTIC · AFRICA · SOUTH AMERICA · OCEAN

Millions of years from now, North and South America will be even further away from Europe and Africa. The Atlantic Ocean will be the biggest.

WE LIVE ON A JIGSAW PUZZLE

The earth's crust is like a puzzle with 12 giant pieces. Each one is a huge plate of rock.

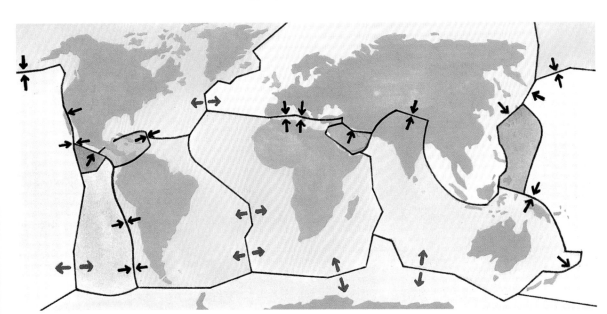

When the plates bump into each other, overlap or rub against each other they cause earthquakes and make mountains and volcanoes.

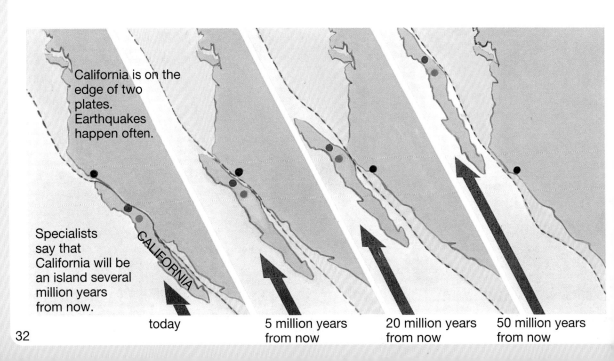

California is on the edge of two plates. Earthquakes happen often.

Specialists say that California will be an island several million years from now.

today

5 million years from now

20 million years from now

50 million years from now

EARTHQUAKE!

Earthquakes can be dangerous when they knock down houses. They often cause fires because gas pipes break when the ground shakes.

When earthquakes are very strong they can crack roads and knock down houses and bridges.

 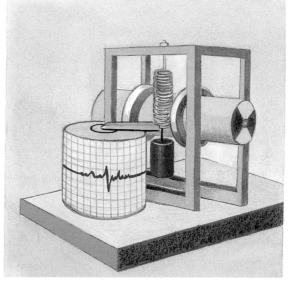

Some houses and buildings are built to resist earthquakes.

Seismographs are used to keep track of and measure earthquakes.

WHEN INDIA MET ASIA

Today, India is part of Asia. But, 135 million years ago India was not part of Asia.

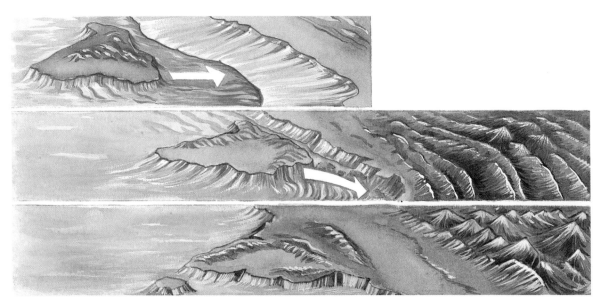

India was far to the south of Asia but the plate it was on moved slowly north. This happened 70 million years ago.

Finally, the Indian plate joined the Asian continent between 30 and 35 million years ago. When the two plates crashed into each other, they created the Himalayas.

THE ROOF OF THE WORLD

Mount Everest is the tallest mountain on Earth. It is 29,028 feet high. It lies on the border between Nepal and Tibet in Asia and is part of the Himalaya mountain range.

On May 29, 1953, Sir Edmund Hillary, from New Zealand, and Tenzing Norgay, a Sherpa, were the first men to climb to the very top of Mt. Everest.

In ancient times, men thought that mountains were the homes of the gods. Tibetans called Mt. Everest Chomo Lungma which means "goddess mother of the world."

YOUNG OR OLD MOUNTAINS?

Look carefully at the mountain tops. If they are high and pointy, the mountains are young. If they are rounded, the mountains are ancient.

Young mountains keep growing very slowly—less than a quarter of an inch per century. They are tall and their slopes are steep.

The tops of these mountains have been worn down by snow, rain, wind and ice. They are very old.

AN ERUPTING VOLCANO

It is so hot in the middle of the earth that rocks melt. The molten rock is liquid and mixes with gases to make the magma that comes out of volcanoes.

Cloud of ash and gas.

Lava comes out of a hole at the top of a volcano called a crater.

The magma that comes out of the crater is called lava.

Lava is a thick liquid that is very hot and red. When it cools it hardens and becomes gray or black.

The earth often growls and gas comes out of the crater before volcanoes erupt. Lava burns everything in its path.

MOUNTAINS OF FIRE

There are more than 10,000 volcanoes on Earth. But only a few hundred are still active.

The mountain Pelée on the island of Martinique in the West Indies completely destroyed the town of St. Pierre in 1902.

Volcanologists can predict when a volcano is going to wake up.

You can find villages at the foot of volcanoes because lava makes the earth very fertile.

THE BIRTH OF A VOLCANO

We very rarely get to see the birth of a volcano. But when we do, it is a fantastic sight! Volcanoes can grow on land or at the bottom of the seas.

In 1943, a farmer in Mexico felt the ground under him shake. The next morning there was a volcano standing in his field!

In 1963, a volcanic island appeared in the middle of a huge jet of dust and burning gas in the middle of the Atlantic Ocean near Iceland. The island was named Surtsey.

PLAINS AND PLATEAUS

Plains and plateaus are large flat spaces. They are often used for farms and ranches.

Wheat and many other grains are grown on the plains.

People raise cattle in the pampas of Argentina.

Plateaus or tablelands are plains high up in the mountains.

Peruvians raise llamas on the plateaus in the Andes mountains.

GLACIERS

It is very, very cold on the tops of mountains and at the poles and the snow does not melt. It slowly clumps together and turns into ice.

When glaciers go over bumps or change direction the ice breaks and a crack forms.

Glaciers are often like huge rivers of ice that move very slowly.

The glaciers at the North and South Poles slide towards the sea and break into huge pieces that float called icebergs. The biggest parts of icebergs are under water. They are dangerous for ships.

WHAT IS A GLACIATED VALLEY?

Glaciers dig valleys in the mountains. The pictures below show how they do this.

First, a stream dug a narrow, V-shaped valley between the mountain sides.

When the climate got colder the snow piled up in the valley and made a glacier.

Millions of years later the earth got warmer and part of the glacier melted. The valley got wider and is now shaped like a U.

EROSION

Water, rain, wind and ice wear down rocks. This changes the landscape and is called "erosion."

Waves eat away at cliffs and pull off hunks of rock.

The rocks, worn down by wind and waves, become pretty pebbles.

The Colorado river has been digging its way through the rocks for thousands of years. Now it flows at the bottom of deep gorges called canyons.

WATER IS A GREAT SCULPTOR!

Throughout the centuries water slowly attacks and eats away at soft rocks. Hard rocks resist erosion better and sometimes take on surprising shapes.

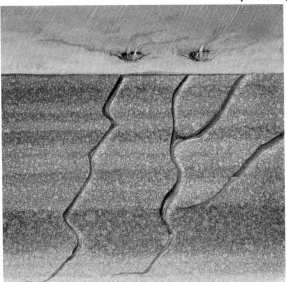

Water wiggles its way in tiny cracks in limestone.

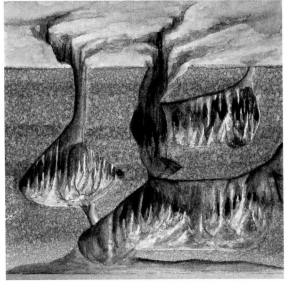

It takes millions of years to dig out caves.

What sculptor could have imagined these extraordinary landscapes in which water created these rock needles?!

DESERTS

When the climate in an area makes it very hard for plants and animals to live it becomes a desert. Deserts can be hot or cold.

Huge cactuses can survive in the American deserts.

There is a very cold desert at the foot of the tallest mountain in the world.

In the desert, the wind blows sand around. When it bumps into a rock it piles up to make a sand dune. They can get very tall.

WHAT IS AN OASIS?

An oasis is a pond of water in the middle of the desert. Date trees and other fruit trees grow around them. Men and animals come to drink the water and quench their thirst.

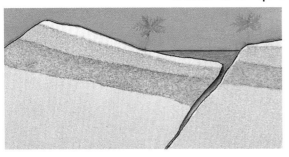 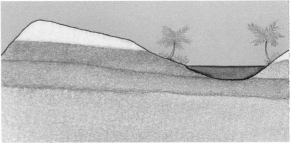

The water held prisoner by underground rocks for millions of years escapes to the surface through cracks in the ground. These natural springs create oases.

A network of canals from the spring or a well irrigates the oasis.
We can then live around the oasis, water gardens, and grow vegetables and grains.

WHERE DOES SAND COME FROM?

Grains of sand are all that is left of rocks that have been worn down over the years.

The seas and rivers rip off bits of rock and wear them down. They become pebbles and then grains of sand.

The sand is gray or black on volcanic beaches.

The sand is bright white on coral beaches.

COASTLINES

All sorts of coastlines are formed when land and sea meet: sandy beaches, rocky coasts, cliffs, etc.

Fjords are ancient glaciated valleys that the sea has taken over.

These huge columns were formed when volcanic rock cooled.

Some coasts have sandy beaches and rocky outcrops side by side.

The wind creates dunes on sandy coastlines.

ISLANDS

There are thousands of islands around the world. Some used to be attached to continents. Others were created when volcanoes erupted in the middle of the ocean.

The sea eats away at the coasts little by little and takes away sand and soft rocks. The land that remains becomes an island surrounded by water.

Volcanoes sprang up in the middle of the Pacific Ocean and created a string of islands, the Galapagos. Iguanas, giant turtles and birds live there.

SALT FIELDS AND POLDERS

On some coasts men have taken over land that used to be under the sea in order to make their countries bigger.

Silt builds up above sea level in some estuaries. The salt goes away over time. The salt fields that are left are good places to raise sheep.

People built dikes in Holland and stole land from the sea. The water is pumped out from inside the dikes to make fields called polders.

UNDERSEA LANDSCAPES

There are plains, plateaus, mountains, volcanoes and deep canyons under the seas.

We build very strong submarines so that we can explore the seas. They are able to withstand the heavy pressure of the water far under the sea.

TREES

Trees are the most important things in the landscapes all over the world. Both men and animals find them useful.

Baobabs and locust trees grow in the savannah.

Trees in equatorial forests wrap their branches around each other.

The Mediterranean coasts are full of pine trees.

Many different animals live in trees.

CHANGING LANDSCAPES

Water, wind and even natural disasters like avalanches, landslides and earthquakes change the landscape.

An avalanche breaks trees and rushes down the mountain side.
A landslide takes part of the hill with it.

Rivers never flow in a straight line. They wander around valleys in loops called meanders. Little by little these loops are worn down by the river and they close up. They leave behind small lakes called oxbow lakes that dry up.

OUR BEAUTIFUL EARTH

Nature has created marvelous and unique landscapes in every country of the world. Earth is full of natural wonders. Follow the pictures on a trip around the world.

The Mediterranean coast is cut by creeks in many places. This makes for lots of rocky inlets.

On the border between Switzerland and Italy lies the Matterhorn. It is 14,691 feet high and one of the tallest in the Alps.

A mountain chain prickled with volcanic peaks lies in the middle of the Sahara desert. It is called the Hoggar Mountains and its highest peak is 9,573 feet tall.

AUSTRALASIA

When you visit Australasia, you can swim in the clear blue waters of the Pacific or meet aborigines in the deserts of Australia.

Look at this Australian desert full of red earth and scraggly plants.

These pointy stones in the north of Australia are really plants surrounded by limestone.

The islands in the Pacific have marvelous white sand beaches and deep blue lagoons where the water is clean and transparent.

ASIA

The longest wall is the world can be found in the middle of this continent. It can even be seen from space!

There are splendid gardens and terraces in China.

Halong Bay in Vietnam is a fantastic sight.

The Great Wall of China is more than 1,500 miles long. It was built by Chinese emperors for protection from invaders.

THE AMERICAS

Don't forget your camera! There are so very many wonderful things to see.

The amazing Grand Canyon in Arizona is 277 miles long and 6,000 feet deep in some places. It was dug by the Colorado River.

The Iguaçu Falls in South America are truly impressive!

Canada has many beautiful lakes and pine and maple forests.

ROCKS

The rocks that can be found under the ground are very useful. Many different kinds are used in buildings.

Granite is a very hard rock that is often used to build houses.

Slate can easily be separated into sheets. It is used to cover roofs because it is waterproof.

You can find the traces and even the remains of animals and plants in limestone. These are fossils.

Early men discovered how to make fire by rubbing pieces of flint together.

NATURAL TREASURES

Beautiful, regularly shaped crystals can be found in rocks. These precious gems come in all different colors.

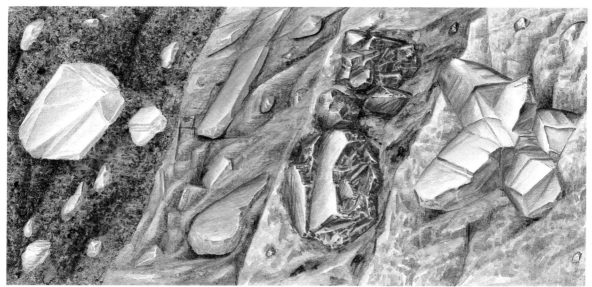

DIAMONDS   EMERALDS   RUBIES   SAPPHIRES

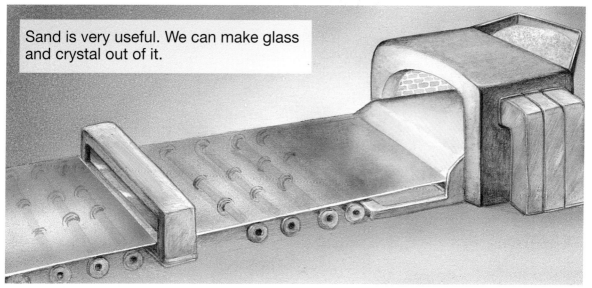

Sand is very useful. We can make glass and crystal out of it.

Factories heat sand in large ovens to make glass. We can add lots of different things to it in order to make it prettier.

UNDERGROUND RICHES

Our planet's basement holds all the riches we use to make many of the things we need.

A very long time ago huge forests found themselves underwater. Little by little the plants decomposed and became thick mud that got buried under layers of rock and turned into coal. Miners remove the coal with machines that pull out chunks of rock.

Plankton is a cloud of microscopic animals and plants that live in the oceans. When they die, they decompose and turn into mud that, when buried under rock, turns into petroleum.

We can get stone, iron, copper, coal, petroleum, the uranium that is used in nuclear power plants and a whole lot more from rocks.

This iron mine was dug in the shape of a stadium with big bleachers by huge mechanical shovels.

EDIBLE ROCKS!

You can make delicious coconut rocks for your friends. For four people you need: 1/2 cup shredded coconut, 1/2 cup sugar and two eggs.

Mix the coconut and the sugar in a large bowl.

Separate the eggs and add the yolks to the coconut and sugar. Mix well.

Beat the egg whites until stiff. Add them to the rest. Mix gently.

Grease a cookie sheet.

Use a small spoon to make "rocks." You can make them in any shape you like!

Get a grown-up to bake them in a hot oven for about 15 minutes.

AN ACCIDENT ON THE COAST

Look carefully at the 6 pictures below. Try to put them in the right order. Remember that the waves wear away the cliffs by crashing into them.

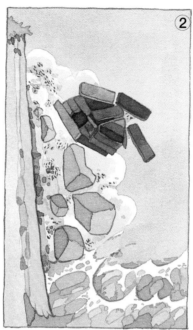

DECORATE YOUR OWN PEBBLES

You can have lots of fun painting smooth stones. Here are a few ideas. What are yours?

a boat

a ladybug

a funny face

Gather smooth round or oval pebbles on the beach. Clean them carefully.

Use a soft lead pencil to draw your pictures on them.

Paint your picture with acrylic paints. You might need to put on two coats of paint.

Once they're dry you can make them shinier by coating them with clear varnish.

WATER AND TIME

SEAS

Seas and oceans are large stretches of salt water. Seas are smaller and often surrounded by land and cut off from the oceans.

The Mediterranean Sea between Europe and Africa is almost completely landlocked.

The Dead Sea is so salty that you don't need to swim. You float!

Some seas freeze over in the winter. Only icebreakers can sail on them then.

Tropical seas are aquatic paradises full of fish and coral.

A PATH FROM SEA TO SEA

More than a hundred years ago a Frenchman, Ferdinand de Lesseps, dug a path from the Mediterranean to the Red Sea. The Suez Canal was to become a busy maritime route.

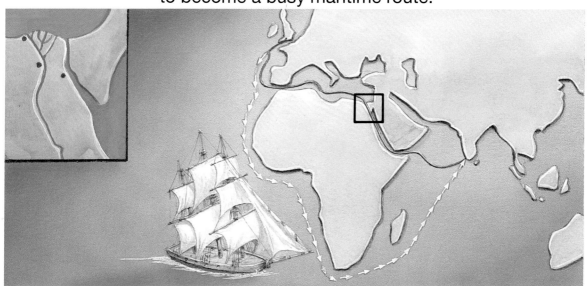

Before, boats had to sail around the Cape of Good Hope on the southern tip of Africa to get to India from Europe. It took 3 long months!

In 1859, digging started. The Suez Canal is over 120 miles long.

Now, it only takes 15 days to sail from Europe to the Orient.

RIVERS ARE VERY USEFUL

They help irrigate the land, supply cities with drinking water and transport men and goods.

Rivers' paths are often dotted with natural obstacles like breaks in the ground that create spectacular waterfalls.

Dams are built to use the force of the water to produce energy.

The Nile River makes it possible for Egyptians to cultivate land in the desert.

The Amazon River is the longest in the world.

The Ganges is a sacred river in India.

FRESH WATER

Fresh water mostly comes from the evaporation of the water in the seas and oceans. It is carried by clouds and falls back to the earth as rain or snow.

The water that flows from glaciers is very pure.

The Amazonian Indians gather water in large leaves. Water is put in bottles in rich countries.

Rivers, lakes, glaciers and underground waterways are the main stores of fresh water on the planet. There is a lot of water available—about 1,000 gallons per day and per person on Earth.

SALT WATER

The water in the oceans became salt water a very long time ago by wearing away rocks. Oceans cover two thirds of Earth so most of the water on the planet is salt water.

Sea water evaporates in salt marshes and leaves behind its salt. The evaporated water is fresh water and turns into clouds.

In some places that used to be covered by the sea there is a thick layer of salt on the ground. Men gather salt to sell there.

WHEN OCEANS AND RIVERS MEET

When a river empties into the sea fresh water mixes with salt water.
Sometimes deltas or lagoons form.

Rivers carry gravel and sand. They sometimes leave them near the riverbanks before emptying into the sea. Little by little arms of earth are formed and stick out into the ocean. This makes a delta where many different animals make their homes.

Mangrove forests grow with their feet in the waters of deltas at the mouths of tropical rivers. Water snakes, birds that go fishing and even fish that climb trees live among the mangrove trees.

LAKES

Lakes are reserves of fresh water. They come in all different sizes and depths. They are fed by underground water streams or by rivers and other waterways.

Some lakes are to be found in giant holes left by earthquakes. These are usually very deep.

Other lakes fill the holes left behind by glaciers.

You can even find lakes in the craters of extinct volcanoes.

GEYSERS

Geysers are spouts of very hot water and steam that shoot out of cracks in the ground at a steady rhythm.

Geyser water comes from rain water that slipped into the ground. It is heated when it gets near burning rocks underground.

TIDES

The ocean rises and falls a few times a day. This movement is called the tides.

When the tide is high the beaches are small. Sometimes they are completely hidden. In the fishing port the boats float on the water.

When it is low tide the beach is bigger and the boats in the port are on dry ground. The high and low tide times change every day.

Tides are caused by both the sun and the moon. They pull on the water in the oceans. The moon is closer to Earth and pulls the hardest.

The tides are very big when the sun and the moon are in line with the earth. In France, at Mont-Saint-Michel, the water goes a long way out and comes back in very fast—as fast as a galloping horse.

Sometimes islands near the coast are linked to the mainland by a road that can only be used when the tide is low.

OCEAN CURRENTS

Currents are like rivers across the seas and oceans. They can be strong or weak. They move warm or cold water.

The strength of the current lets baby turtles swim effortlessly and carries coconuts far away from their trees.

We could even cross the ocean on a raft in the right current.

A warm current lets palm trees grow in the south of England.

WAVES

When the wind blows on the sea it makes waves. The longer and harder it blows, the bigger the waves.

Surfers look for big waves to ride. They slip inside the tunnels made by waves.

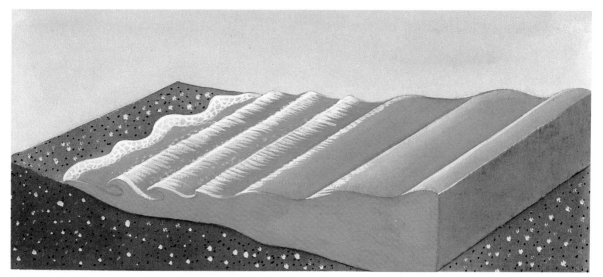

Waves form out at sea and break against the shore. Sometimes there are waves even when there is no wind. These waves are caused by storms thousands of miles away.

THE RICHES OF THE SEA

Man has long used the riches of the seas. We fish and collect seashells and seaweed.

The trawler above is dragging a huge net behind it called a trawl net. Fishermen use computers to find schools of fish.

We get oil from under the sea. We also use the movement of the tides to make electricity and use sand and gravel to build houses.

Dragnets are used to gather sand and gravel.

This brown seaweed called wrack is used in some foods.

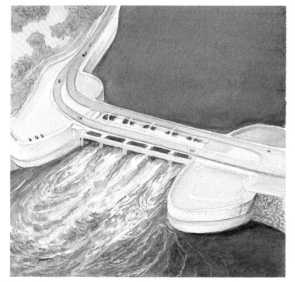

The movement of water can be made into electricity.

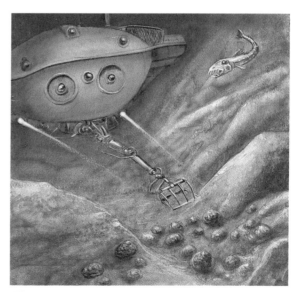

The ocean floor is rich in metal.

REEF BUILDERS

Coral is not rock. It is made up of tiny animals that live in warm waters. They make limestone shells. Thousands and thousands gather together and make coral reefs.

Brightly colored fish move about in this superb underwater garden made of different coral shapes.

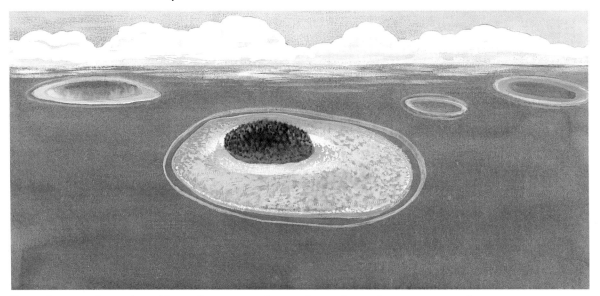

Coral attaches itself to the round peaks of underwater volcanoes. You can see a ring of coral called an atoll on the surface.

SEA FARMING

People raise oysters, mussels and fish in farms in order to save the sea's resources. They are the farmers of the sea.

Mussels grow on wooden posts called mussel beds.

Oysters grow on steel sheets or tubes.

Salmon and trout are grown in tanks.

In Asia, people grow seaweed to eat.

WATER'S GREAT VOYAGE

Water rises to the sky (as water vapor), falls to Earth as rain and returns to the seas in rivers. This is the water cycle.

The water that falls to Earth can do many things: evaporate right away, sink into the ground, fill rivers and streams that carry it to the seas and oceans, or be captured by man for his needs. Water is used in homes and factories but it goes back to the rivers and seas through sewer systems which collect used water. Thus, water is constantly traveling.

A lot of the water that sinks into the ground is absorbed by the roots of plants. The rest either returns to the surface as springs or goes straight back to the seas.

RAIN, SNOW AND HAIL

Millions of tons of water float over our heads in clouds. It falls to Earth in the form of rain, snow and hail.

▼ When it is very cold, the tiny drops of water in the clouds freeze. They stick together and make snow flakes that fall to Earth.

▲ Clouds are made of very tiny drops of water. When they bump into each other they stick together and get bigger. When they are heavy enough it rains.

◄ Sometimes when the air is very cold small pieces of ice stick together and make hail— different sized balls of ice. Heavy hail storms can do lots of damage.

OUR CHANGING SKY

The color of the sky changes with the seasons and the clouds that float across it. The summer sky is usually blue but it can get dark very quickly if there's a storm brewing.

◀ When the sun's rays shine at an angle through a curtain of rain the light breaks up into seven colors: red, orange, yellow, green, blue, indigo and purple. This makes a rainbow.

▼ Fog is a cloud spread out across the ground or water. It is made when damp air cools down.

▲ The air is agitated at the end of a very hot day. Drops of air in the clouds rise and fall and pick up electricity. This causes thunder and lightening.

TEMPESTS

Tempests occur when the wind is very, very strong. Waves get bigger and slam violently into the coasts.

Air currents—wind—form when hot air (which is lighter) meets cold air (which is heavier).

Big waves are tossing this ship about! It can no longer be controlled. Sometimes the crew and passengers have to be evacuated by helicopter or in lifeboats.

VIOLENT WINDS

Violent winds called cyclones form over the oceans in the summer in some warm areas.

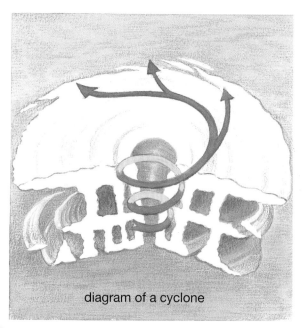

diagram of a cyclone

There is no wind or rain in the center—called the eye—of cyclones. The eye is surrounded by walls of rain-filled clouds in which winds blow at more than 180 miles per hour. Cyclones move slowly (between 12 and 20 miles per hour) and destroy everything in their paths. Cyclones sometimes cause tidal waves.

Tornadoes are very violent winds that spin about. These giant funnels form in clouds. Tornadoes can suck up everything in their paths—houses, trees and even the water in a pond. The wind inside the cloud can move very fast—between 300 and 650 miles per hour!

THE OCEANS ARE IN DANGER

Our seas and oceans are threatened by pollution. You can help protect them by never leaving any garbage on the beach.

Sewers empty into rivers or the ocean.

Beaches are often littered with garbage.

When oil tankers have accidents huge layers of oil spill into the sea. Oil spills are sometimes called oil slicks. They kill hundreds of birds and fish.

LIFE ON EARTH

LIFE BEGAN IN THE OCEAN

Nothing lived on Earth when it was first formed, more than 4.5 billion years ago. The first signs of life appeared in warm seas.

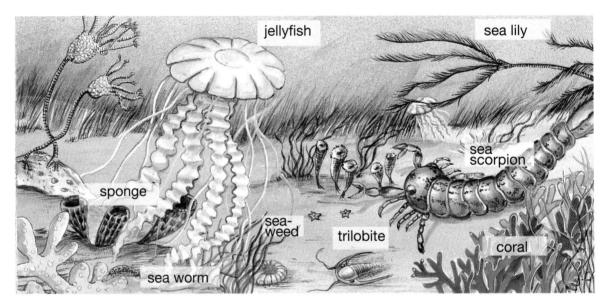

First came seaweed, then sea worms, then coral. Next came sponges, jellyfish and sea animals that had shells (sea urchins, sea scorpions and trilobites).

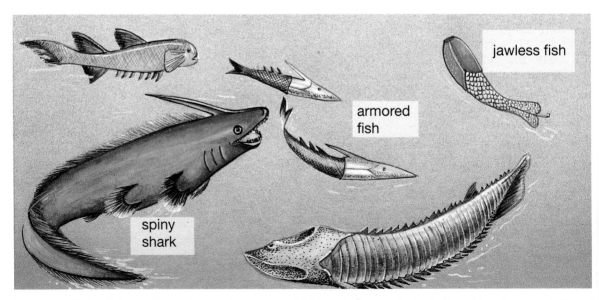

The first fish did not have jaws, just round holes for mouths. Spiny sharks were the first fish to have jaws. Armored fish were covered with bony shells.

TRACES OF THE PAST

Scientists can piece together the earth's past thanks to the traces that plants and animals left in rocks.

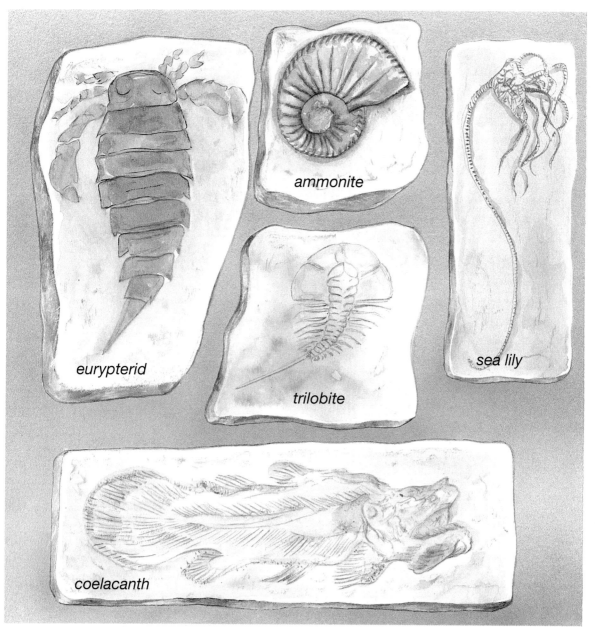

eurypterid

ammonite

trilobite

sea lily

coelacanth

All these animals lived in the sea. Some, like the coelacanth, are still around today. It first appeared 300 million years ago, well before the dinosaurs.

OUT OF THE WATER!

350 million years ago some fish left the water for land. They became amphibians. These animals live both on land and in water.

The ichthyosaur was the first amphibian to walk on land. Its thick, finned tail let it swim very quickly when in the water.

Later, 250 million years ago, reptiles appeared. Flying reptiles filled the sky and dinosaurs ruled the earth.

WHY DID THE DINOSAURS DISAPPEAR?

Dinosaurs disappeared very suddenly around 65 million years ago.
Scientists wonder why. Below are a few possibilities.

A huge volcanic eruption or a giant meteorite might have created a very
hot cloud of ash that hid the sun for several months. This would have
killed off the plants and animals.

The climate might have become colder,
killing the plants. The dinosaurs would
have died of hunger.

The climate might have got hotter,
drying up most of the water and killing
many plants.

MAMMALS RULE!

When the dinosaurs died off 65 million years ago the mammals that were living hidden in the forest multiplied, got bigger and took over the earth.

Megatheriums were 9 feet tall and ate plants.
Glyptodonts had 9-foot long shells to protect them.

Mammoths lived 2 million years ago during the ice age. Cave bears and woolly rhinoceroses lived at the same time.

THE FIRST PLANTS

Seaweed invaded the land millions and millions of years ago.
They gave birth to other plants such as mosses, lichens and ferns.

Seaweed, moss and lichen do not have real roots. They have small,
cleat-like roots that let them hold on to the ground.

Giant plants developed in the first forests. Some are still around today
but they are much smaller.

TREES AND FLOWERS APPEAR

Earth was covered with huge forests in the dinosaur age. New flowers appeared everywhere.

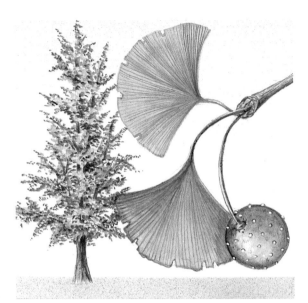

The ginkgo tree appeared before the dinosaurs and still exists.

Magnolias were some of the very first flowers.

The first roses developed millions of years later.

Once the dinosaurs were gone flowers spread all over.

THE FIRST MEN

The animals that would later become men appeared in Africa 3.5 million years ago. They spread all over the world.

Australopithecus ate leaves and fruit. They lived on the ground and in trees.

Homo habilis hunted all kinds of animals. They used stone knives to cut them up.

Homo erectus discovered how to make fire by rubbing two pieces of flint together. This let them cook their food, make weapons and protect themselves from wild animals.

OUR ANCESTORS

Homo erectus, the first real humans, were followed by homo sapiens. All the people on Earth are their descendants.

Neanderthal man hunted mammoths and buffalo. They used their skins to make clothes and cover the huts they built.

Cro-Magnon man had a well-developed language. They carved statues out of bone and painted hunting scenes on the walls of caves.

ANTARCTIC ANIMALS

The Antarctic is the coldest place on Earth. Seals, walruses and whales all have a thick layer of fat that protects them from the extreme cold.

Penguins live in colonies. The daddy penguin sits on the egg for two months to protect it from the cold.

Seals spend most of their time under the ice.

Blue whales are the largest animals on Earth. They weigh about 150 tons.

ARCTIC ANIMALS

Polar bears and seals live on ice fields. Polar foxes, Arctic hares and musk oxen can be found in Arctic areas that are not covered by ice all year round.

Polar bears catch seals with one swipe of a paw.

Polar foxes are excellent hunters.

Musk oxen have long, thick fleece to protect them from the cold.

Terns are tireless travelers. They fly close to 10,000 miles per year.

AMAZONIAN FOREST ANIMALS

The flora and fauna amongst the interwoven vines of the tropical forests of the Amazon are the most varied in the world.

1 - Monkey spider. 2 - The macaw is the largest parakeet in South America.
3 - Toucan. 4 - Green boa. 5 - Sloth. 6 - Jaguar. 7 - Giant armadillo.

DESERT ANIMALS

It is very hot during the day and cold at night in the deserts.
All desert animals can get by with very little water.

Camels can go several weeks without drinking thanks to their fat-filled humps.

Addax antelopes never drink. They get all the water they need from the plants they eat.

desert cat

jerboa

horned viper

desert turtle

fennec

desert hedgehog

scorpion

Animals in the desert hide from the sun and heat. Fennecs and hedgehogs slip into holes in rocks or in dens. Horned vipers bury themselves in the sand.

MOUNTAIN ANIMALS

Animals that live in the mountains know how to protect themselves from the cold. Some hibernate in the winter, others change their fur.

Marmots stuff themselves with grass before sleeping for the winter.

Bears give birth to two or three bear cubs in January or February.

Chamois and ibex have hooves that are good for climbing.

In wintertime, ermines' fur becomes all white.

FOREST ANIMALS

Lots of animals live in this forest. Can you find them all? There is a fawn, a stag, a badger, a squirrel, a fox, a boar, an owl, a porcupine and a weasel.

Forests in temperate regions are homes to many different animals. They can be hard to find because many of them only come out at night.

ANIMALS IN THE SAVANNAH

Wild cats and large herds of herbivores live in the great plains of Africa. During the dry season, whole herds of animals migrate to areas where they can find water and grass.

Giraffes can eat the leaves on the tops of trees because of their long necks.

Elephants spray water on their bodies with their trunks to cool off.

Lions sleep most of the day. They hunt at night.

Cheetahs can run faster than any other animal on Earth. They can go as fast as 60 mph.

Here are a few savannah animals: a lion (1), a cheetah (2), a zebra (3), a gazelle (4), a giraffe (5) and an elephant (6).

SEA ANIMALS

The picture below shows lots of different sea animals all together.
In reality, they do not all live in the same place.

1. Dolphin, 2. Whale, 3. Shark, 4. Sea anemone, 5. Mussels, 6. Crab,
7. Octopus, 8. Coral, 9. Deep water fish.

ENDANGERED SPECIES

Lots of animals are in danger of dying out because mankind often hunts them too much and pollutes or destroys their natural habitat. Certain animal species are now protected.

Siberian tigers have been hunted for their fur too much. They are slowly disappearing. There are only about 300 left.

Siberian tiger

The okapi is in danger of dying out because it is very rare. It belongs to the giraffe family.

okapi

Cheetahs are in danger because their natural habitat, the savannah, is disappearing and because they are still hunted for their fur.

cheetah

otter

monk seal

European mink

The Hawaiian monk seal is slowly disappearing. They can no longer visit the beaches where they used to get their food because they have been invaded by tourists.

Otters are becoming rarer and rarer in rivers and marshes. They are victims of water pollution.

There are very few European minks left. They have not survived the drying up of marshes and the pollution of rivers.

LONG GONE!

Certain animals have been hunted down by men and have disappeared from the face of the earth.

① The quagga, a type of zebra, used to live in Africa.

② Farmers exterminated Tasmanian wolves to protect their herds.

③ Dodos were all eaten by sailors that landed on the island where they lived.

④ These large penguins were killed by hunters. Their feathers were used for pillows and mattresses.

⑤ Moas, distant cousins of ostriches, were massacred by hunters for their meat.

PROTECTED SPECIES

Huge natural parks have been created in order to prevent more animals from disappearing. There, animals can live and reproduce in a natural habitat where they are protected from hunters.

The lynx, the buffalo, the ibex and the wolf are now protected animals. They are released into natural parks where they are watched over. Men verify that they adapt to the park and that they reproduce.

PROTECTED FLOWERS

Today, many flowers are in danger of disappearing too. They have been gathered too much, crushed and destroyed by insecticides. Laws have been passed to protect some of them. They can not be picked.

Endangered flowers: 1. water lily, 2. hibiscus, 3. orchid, 4. poppy, 5. papyrus, 6. cornflower, 7. gentian.

QUICK QUESTIONS

Can you remember the answers to these questions? If not, look back at the beginning of the book.

A volcanic island surrounded by a coral reef is called:
– a fjord
– an atoll
– a polder

The longest river in the world is:
– the Rhine
– the Nile
– the Amazon

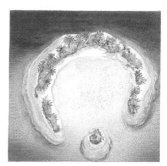

A delta is:
– an undersea volcano
– a river in Asia
– strips of land that stretch into the ocean
– an ocean current

Wrack is:
– precious metal
– seaweed
– a type of coral
– a fish

A Cyclone is:
– a spinning storm
– a fast-moving cloud
– a hail storm

LIFE IN ASIA

Half of the people on Earth live in Asia. Much of Asia has a damp climate and fertile lands.

Above, women are picking tea leaves in India.

Indians bathe in the sacred waters of the Ganges.

Indians weave beautiful cotton cloth.

Millions of Chinese families raise silk worms.

There are many big industrial cities in Japan but in the rest of Asia many people live on farms. The wide Siberian plains in the north are almost empty. More people live in China (in the center) than in any other country in the world.

Above, people are planting rice in a rice paddy in Vietnam.

Tokyo is the second largest city in the world. Its subways are crowded.

Above is a picture of a floating market in Bangkok.

Many nomads live in tents on the Siberian plains.

LIFE IN EUROPE

This small continent is full of people. Each country has its own customs, language and way of life.

In winter, young Norwegians use skis to get around.

Holland is famous for its beautiful tulip fields.

Tourists from all over the world admire the Eiffel Tower in Paris.

Cars and buses drive on the left side of the road in London.

Life in England is very different from life in Greece or Russia! More and more Europeans live in cities. The countrysides are emptying.

German factories produce thousands of tons of steel.

Switzerland, high in the mountains, has many mountain pastures.

Bullfights are still a popular tradition in Spain.

Russian children ice-skate on the frozen river in Saint Petersburg.

LIFE IN THE AMERICAS

What a lot there is to see on these two continents, from the modern cities in North America to the beautiful West Indies and the coffee and sugar plantations in South America!

People of all different nationalities live in New York.

Canadian rivers carry tree trunks from their rich forests.

The space shuttle is launched in Cape Canaveral.

Inuits hunt and fish in the Great White North.

Eskimos, Incas and the last Native Americans share their continents with the descendants of Africans and Europeans that fill the land.

In North America, farmers cultivate huge fields.

In the Amazon forests, Indians hunt for food.

In Brazil, many families make their living with sugar cane.

Huge plantations produce coffee in Colombia.

LIFE IN AFRICA

Men have filled the areas where farming and ranching are possible on this continent, the hottest in the world.

The Tuareg tribe in North Africa raise camels and goats.

Here, women are crushing grain—millet and cassava.

Dakar is a huge port city in Senegal.

Merchants are selling jewelry, copper, carpets and cloth in this souk.

Only nomads live in the deserts. Many Africans live in small villages.
They hunt, fish, grow cassava, citrus fruits, cocoa, cotton and more.
There are not many big cities yet.

Pygmies are a small people that
live in the equatorial forests.

There are gold and diamond
mines in many areas.

The largest city in Africa is Cairo,
the capital of Egypt.

Some houses are made of earthen
bricks.

LIFE IN AUSTRALASIA

Australia, New Zealand, New Guinea and the neighboring islands of the Pacific are all in Australasia. Australia, the largest island in the world, has

Sydney is the largest and oldest city in Australia.

Trucks and trains carry animals and other goods.

Australian beaches are full of people playing sports.

The first inhabitants of Australia were aborigines.

a small population—the center of the country is full of deserts. Many Australians live in large, sunny cities on the shores of the Pacific.

People in Polynesia live mostly from fishing.

There are many sheep ranches in New Zealand.

The inhabitants of many Pacific islands have kept their traditions.

Huge, mysterious stone statues stand on Easter Island.

POPULATIONS OF THE WORLD

There are lots of people in some countries and very few in others. Look closely at the continents. Can you point to the continent with the largest population? With the smallest?

ASIA: 3,392 million people (one out of two people on Earth is Asian).

EUROPE: 728 million people.

North and South AMERICA: 760 million people.

AFRICA: 700 million people.

AUSTRALASIA: 28 million people.

There are more than 5.6 billion people on Earth!

CHILDREN AROUND THE WORLD

Children live differently all around the world. Some live in hot countries, others in cold countries.

◄ In India children like flying kites.

▲ Eskimos ride snow-bikes in winter.

◄ Chinese children often study calligraphy.

Schools in Africa are often outdoors. ▶

Baseball is very popular in America. ▶

▲ Children in the Pacific islands row canoes.

GAMES AND SPORTS

Depending on which country they live in, children prefer different games and sports.

These girls in Tahiti are making flower necklaces.

These Japanese boys are studying karate.

These European children and having fun in a playground.

These Australians have fun surfing and wind surfing.

In Brazil, these boys are playing soccer.

This Tuareg boy is learning how to ride a camel.

SOME CHILDREN'S LIVES ARE DIFFICULT

Children in many poor countries have to go to work to help support their families.

1 – Children are at work in transporting ore in a mine in South America.

2 – Children from shantytowns search for even the smallest piece of metal or plastic in garbage dumps. They will sell them for recycling.

3 – This African boy gets up early to watch over a flock of goats.

4 – Children in Amazonian tribes learn how to hunt and fish with a bow or a spear very early.

HOUSES AROUND THE WORLD

Houses are different all over the world. Some are made of wood, others are made of earth or concrete.

Many houses in Canada are made of wood.

Houses in Greece are often whitewashed.

Some huts in Africa have walls of clay and palm leaf roofs.

Many houses in Asia are built on stilts.

Each country builds different kinds of buildings depending on its climate, weather and the materials that are to be found there.

Huge skyscrapers fill the streets of New York.

Many buildings in Africa are made out of bricks of dried earth.

Nomads live in big tents in the deserts.

In mountain areas there are lots of wooden cottages called chalets.

POOR COUNTRIES

Most poor countries are in the south. Much of Africa and even large countries like India are among the poorest in the world.

richer countries

poorer countries

People do not always have enough to eat in poor countries. Farms are often destroyed by too much or not enough rain. Many cities are surrounded by shantytowns that are filled with poor people that have fled the countrysides.

RICH COUNTRIES

The industrialized countries in the north of our planet such as the United States, Japan and countries in Europe are the richest. Their wealth comes from agriculture and especially industry and commerce.

The richest countries have many factories. They produce airplanes, cars, computers, televisions and many more things. Their cities have huge stores where you can find everything you could want.

THE EARTH IS IN DANGER

The biggest threat to the earth is nuclear war. If we were crazy enough to set off a nuclear war, everything could be destroyed—plants, animals and even mankind.

Populations and animal farming are increasing near the deserts. Trees and grasses are disappearing and the deserts are growing.

We throw away tons of plastic containers. They fill garbage cans and increase the size of garbage dumps.

Chemical fertilizers get into the ground and pollute the water supply.

This huge mushroom cloud is caused by a nuclear bomb that destroys everything for hundreds of miles around it.

The population is growing and we need more and more houses and factories. Man's race for life is putting the earth in danger.

This old pipeline across Siberia is leaking in several places. The escaping oil has caught fire and is burning the surrounding earth. Flora and fauna are dying in this polluted pond.

Tourist beaches are lined with lots of buildings. These concrete walls have destroyed plants and forests.

The Aral Sea is becoming a desert because the 2 rivers that fed it have been turned aside. It will have disappeared in 20 years.

ENDANGERED EARTH

Mankind can do a lot of damage to nature. If we do not protect our countrysides, forests and rivers, life on Earth will be threatened.

Chemical factories give off poisonous gasses that fall to Earth as acid rain and kill trees.

The land on the edges of the Nile is treated with chemical fertilizers. Because of them, the river has been invaded by hyacinths.

Men cut down tropical forests. This leaves the ground bare and the soil is carried away by wind and rain. Barren earth is left.

One lit cigarette butt can cause a giant forest fire. It takes years for the trees to grow back.

ISBN 2-215-06242-8
© Éditions FLEURUS, Paris, 1999.
Printed in Italy.